Little Grey Rabbit's Paint-Box

The Little Grey Rabbit Library

Little Grey Rabbit's Paint-Box

Alison Uttley

pictures by Margaret Tempest

Collins

William Collins Sons & Co Ltd
London · Glasgow · Sydney · Auckland
Toronto · Johannesburg

First published 1958
© text The Alison Uttley Literary Property Trust 1986
© illustrations The Estate of Margaret Tempest 1986
© this arrangement William Collins Sons & Co Ltd 1986
Second impression 1987
Cover decoration by Fiona Owen
Decorated capital by Mary Cooper
Alison Uttley's original story has been abridged for this book.
Uttley, Alison
Little Grey Rabbit's Paint-Box. —
Rev. ed. — (Little Grey Rabbit books)
I. Title   II. Tempest, Margaret
III. Series
823'.912 [J] PZ7

ISBN 0-00-194212-3

Made and printed in Great Britain by
William Collins Sons and Co Ltd, Glasgow

FOREWORD

Of course you must understand that Grey Rabbit's home had no electric light or gas, and even the candles were made from pith of rushes dipped in wax from the wild bees' nests, which Squirrel found. Water there was in plenty, but it did not come from a tap. It flowed from a spring outside, which rose up from the ground and went to a brook. Grey Rabbit cooked on a fire, but it was a wood fire, there was no coal in that part of the country. Tea did not come from India, but from a little herb known very well to country people, who once dried it and used it in their cottage homes. Bread was baked from wheat ears, ground fine, and Hare and Grey Rabbit gleaned in the cornfields to get the wheat.

The doormats were plaited rushes, like country-made mats, and cushions were stuffed with wool gathered from the hedges where sheep pushed through the thorns. As for the looking-glass, Grey Rabbit found the glass, dropped from a lady's handbag, and Mole made a frame for it. Usually the animals gazed at themselves in the still pools as so many country children have done. The country ways of Grey Rabbit were the country ways known to the author.

Hare was lolloping quietly over a field one fine day when he saw a lady sitting on a little stool in the grass. She was busy with a white book and a black box with something nice within. Hare was most astonished, for it was his favourite meadow. He took shelter behind a crooked hawthorn and watched her.

"What is she doing?" he whispered to the bumble-bees, but they never answered at all, for they were busy too.

The lady went on with her work painting the hills, the end of a barn, the hawthorn and the blue sky above. She saw Mr Hare peeping at her, and, smiling to herself, she drew his long ears and round face in her sketchbook.

After some time she placed the open book on a rock near her; she yawned and stretched herself.

"That's enough," she murmured. "I'll have lunch while it dries."

She went to the low wall, took some sandwiches from a case, and stayed there, eating her lunch, looking across the valley.

Hare ran quickly over the grass to find out what she had been doing.

"Green-grass-making," said he, and he touched the picture with the tip of his tongue.

"Nasty taste," he grunted. Then he saw himself, a little brown hare with two long ears and a bright eye.

"That's me, in the looking-glass," he cried, and he tucked the sketch-book under his arm, and ran very fast.

When the lady came back she could not believe her book had vanished. She hunted everywhere, and at last, puzzled and bewildered, she went away.

"Look what I've found," cried Hare, as he dashed into the little house where Squirrel and Grey Rabbit were sewing.

"What is it? A big toadstool?" asked Squirrel.

"A book?" asked Grey Rabbit.

Hare placed the sketch-book open upon the table, with a proud air.

"Cowslip Meadow and you peeping from behind our tree," said Squirrel, touching it gingerly with her paw.

"Hare, is it really you?" exclaimed Grey Rabbit.

"I watched a lady do it," said Hare, leaping up and down. "I was hiding behind a tree, but she got me and put me here."

"Oh Hare. she didn't hurt you, did she?" asked Grey Rabbit, tenderly.

"No Grey Rabbit. I felt nothing except an ache with keeping still so long. I waited till she moved away. She left this book. People often leave things behind them."

"Yes," agreed Squirrel. "There was that pink hanky Grey Rabbit made into a nightcap."

"And a crooked sixpence Moldy Warp found," added Grey Rabbit. "People leave

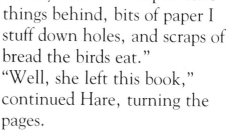

things behind, bits of paper I stuff down holes, and scraps of bread the birds eat."

"Well, she left this book," continued Hare, turning the pages.

"No writing," said Grey Rabbit. "Only pictures. A pretty book."

"Here's Wise Owl's tree," said Grey Rabbit. "She hasn't seen Wise Owl's bell and his door."

"She doesn't go very near," explained Hare. "She doesn't notice all the leaves and ladybirds and insects."

So they flipped the pages over with their furry paws, and gazed at pictures of fields and trees, with an occasional cottage, and the hills in the distance.

When Milkman Hedgehog came the next day with the cans of milk they invited him indoors and showed him the strange book.

"Aye, it's that lady-artist, staying at the farm," said Old Hedgehog at once. "I knows her by sight. She's always in the fields. She means no harm, but when I tasted some of the paint in her box, all in tidy little flat cakes, I felt very poorly. I was real badly. You didn't eat any, did you, Mr Hare?"

"No, I only took a lick of the picture. The box was shut," said Hare, thankful he had escaped. "I had to hurry off with the book; she left it on a stone."

"You ought not to have took it, Mr Hare," said Hedgehog, gravely. "She left it to dry. I've seen her do that before."

"You must take it back, Hare," said Grey Rabbit.

Hare pouted. "Finding's keeping."

"You can't find if it isn't lost," said Squirrel.

"Yes, I can," cried Hare, quickly. "I find lots of things, snail shells, jay's blue feathers, striped pebbles, green acorns, and none of 'em is lost. This old book isn't lost, it's left."

"Now, take it back, do, Mr Hare," said Old Hedgehog.

"Let me show everybody first," pleaded Hare, and Grey Rabbit agreed.

So Hare ran out to show the pictures to Moldy Warp the Mole.

"They are not as lasting as that Roman picture I once saw deep in the earth," said the Mole. "If you left these out in the rain for a day they would melt away, they would run."

"That was made of stone, a dolphin," answered Hare.

"You and Grey Rabbit could paint if you tried," continued the Mole, rubbing a picture with his little hand.

"How?" asked Hare.

"Oh, you have a brush, and you paint," said Mole, airily. "Very easy."

"A hearth-brush? A sweeping-brush? A besom? A clothes-brush?" cried Hare.

"No, nor a Fox's brush," laughed Moldy Warp. "A thin brush, made of a feather, or hair, or even your own paw, Hare. It's hairy and soft. It would be good for big things like fields."

"Do you really mean it, Moldy Warp?" Hare leapt on top of the mole-hill and down again.

"Of course you can, Grey Rabbit too, and Squirrel. All artists."

Hare danced away with the sketchbook, singing loudly for all to hear.

"I'm going to be an artist, an artist-fellow;
I'm going to paint a picture,
red and blue and yellow."

He leaped away to find the Speckledy Hen. There was a picture of her in the book.

"What did you say, Hare? Me? That's not me," cried the flustered Hen. She pecked the sketch of a fat little hen feeding in the farmyard; her sharp beak tore a hole in the paper.

"It's not me," she spluttered, cackling loudly. "It doesn't speak or move. You could paint a better picture yourself, Hare."

"Could I?" asked Hare.

"Take one of my feathers and try," said the Hen and she pulled out a feather and gave it to Hare.

So Hare hurried away delighted, to find little Fuzzypeg. Fuzzypeg was not impressed. "It's not as nice as my book of Fables I once read to the Fox. Will you show it to the Fox, Hare?" he asked.

"No," said Hare, shortly, and then he started, for the Fox was watching him.

"Let me look," said the Fox sternly, and he stepped leisurely from the edge of the wood and straightened his red jacket.

"A book?" he continued. "I like books, especially picture books. Am I in it?"

"No," spluttered Hare. "N-n-not yet."

The Fox turned the pages. "Hare and a duck and a fat hen, and some rabbits," he murmured. "A good supper. I'm hungry."

He looked intently at Hare, but Hare took out his watch.

"Not dinner-time yet," said Hare. "Not quite supper-time, either." He shook his watch and they both listened.

"Tick Tack, Tick Tack," said the watch, more loudly than usual, and the Fox, who did not like ticking noises, moved away.

"I'm going to be an artist," said Hare, boldly. "So is Grey Rabbit. I will paint a picture of you, Mr Fox."

"I'll give you a bit of my brush," said the Fox, and he pulled out a few red hairs from his tail, tied them together and presented them to Hare.

"Mind you make it like me," said he.

Hare went on his way, very thoughtful now. He showed the book to the gipsy's horse grazing on the common, for the caravan and horse and gipsy were all sketched in bright colours.

Duke whinnied with pleasure.

"You can have your picture," said Hare, tearing it out. "You took us to the seaside when we had the sneezes."

"Thank you, kindly," answered Duke. "Pin it in the caravan, Hare. My master's asleep. He will be pleased."

So Hare pinned the picture to a blanket. Then he went on his way to the river where Water-rat was dreamily rowing his boat, singing to himself.

"Hi! Water-rat!" called Hare. "Come here!"

Water-rat tied the little skiff to a reed and swam ashore.

"A book? Is it Wise Owl's?" he asked.

"No. Made by an artist. Pictures in it. River and fields and me," said Hare.

"My river," said Water-rat, as he looked at the scene. "But it is too dry."

He poured a little river water over it.

"It belongs to a lady," Hare told him.

"I remember her," returned Water-rat. "She threw me a sandwich one day."

He stared hard at the picture. Then he broke off a flowering-rush, searched for a patch of reddish mud, and, using the rush as a paint brush, he skilfully sketched a little boat on the river with himself at the oars.

"That's how it should be," said he. "Keep the brush. You and Squirrel and Grey Rabbit can paint with it. Use mud and wood-ash and honey."

"Thank you," said Hare, doubtfully.

"You must show this to Wise Owl. Here's his tree," said Water-rat.

"I suppose I must," sighed Hare. "I 'specks he'll eat it all."

He went reluctantly to the wood with the damp sketch-book under his arm.

"Tinkle! Tinkle!" rang the little silver bell. There was a shuffle aloft and Hare pulled the bell again.

"Don't ring twice!" hooted the Owl, crossly. "Who's there? Go away whoever you are. Too-whit! Too-whoo!"

"It's me! Hare! I've got a book," called Hare, shakily.

"A book? Is it for me?" Wise Owl came to the door, wide awake with sudden interest.

"It belongs to an artist. There's your tree in it," shouted Hare.

Wise Owl dropped silently down to the tree roots and turned the pages, muttering and mumbling to himself.

"Yes, it's my tree, all right," said he. "No bell, no door, no owl. Not safe."

He tore out the picture, and swallowed it. Then, with the sketch-book in his beak he flew back and disappeared.

"Oh dear!" groaned Hare. "He's going to eat everything. Just as I feared."

Hare waited with a sinking heart.

Suddenly the book fluttered down, and with it a parcel and a feather.

"Take your old book, Hare," hissed Wise Owl. "Here's a paint box and a brush for Grey Rabbit. Let her try. I've added my picture to the collection."

The brush was made of Wise Owl's breast feathers, soft as a shadow, and the leaf-covered box was tied with looped grass.

Hare hurried home after that, eager to show Wise Owl's presents. He flung the bedraggled book on the table with the small brush and the green box, and he sank exhausted in the rocking-chair.

Squirrel and Grey Rabbit turned the damp pages.

They found the nice little boat painted in river-mud, and the hole the Speckledy Hen had made, and the marks where two pages had been torn out. Then, on a nice clean page they discovered Wise Owl's picture. It was signed with a large O, so they knew it was Wise Owl's picture.

"The full moon," whispered Squirrel.

The beautiful golden moon shone on the page, lighting up the whole room. Around spread the deep blue sky, covering the page.

"He has painted his best friend," murmured Grey Rabbit. "The moon and Wise Owl go together."

Grey Rabbit picked up the soft painting brush, and stroked her cheek with it. Then she opened the green-leaf box.

"Oh! Oh!" she cried. "It's a paint box for me. It has me on the lid, but of course, you can all use it."

There was a row of little paints inside – blue from the violet, pink from the wild rose, yellow from the cowslip, purple from the grasses, grey from the shadows and black from the night.

"He has made these himself," said Grey Rabbit. "I must take him a present."

"Make him a picture," said Hare.

"I can only paint little earth things, not a moon or stars or sun," replied Grey Rabbit.

Hare took the sketch-book back to the field and placed it carefully on the rock.

"Won't she be surprised when she sees Wise Owl's picture!" said he to himself. "I wish we could have kept it."

He waited behind the tree, nibbling the grass, smelling the scents, until the lady appeared with a friend.

"I left it on that rock," said she. "Oh there's something white! Can it be? Yes, it is. It is my lost book."

She hurried across the grass, and picked it up with cries of astonishment.

"Two pages torn out, and look! A little boat on the river with a water-rat!"

Then she gave a gasp of amazement.

"Here's the moon! It shines! This is pure magic! Who can have done it?"

Hare rolled on the grass with laughter, then went gallumping home to tell the tale.

Squirrel and Grey Rabbit were busy, painting on strips of silver-birch bark which Squirrel had gathered. Grey Rabbit used the feather brush of Wise Owl, Squirrel had the flowering rush, so Hare joined them and painted with Speckledy Hen's ragged feather and his own soft paw, and the hairy brush from the Fox.

They worked so hard they forgot to have tea, and they were still painting when the moon rose in the sky. Wise Owl flew over: he peered through the window at the three small animals; he tapped at the pane with his beak.

"Too-whit! Too-whee! Any pictures for me?" he called.

So they put down their brushes and showed their work.

Squirrel had painted a dish of cakes, pink cakes and red cakes, cream buns and plum cake, for she thought Wise Owl would enjoy them. They looked as good as real ones.

Grey Rabbit had made a picture of the little house at night, with the candle shining through the window, and Wise Owl flying over the roof.

Hare had painted a picture of the Fox, with his red hair on end and his mouth open, and who should be riding on his back but Hare himself! Hare held a long stick in his paw, and he guided Mr Fox with reins.

Squirrel and Grey Rabbit laid their paintings on the grass outside, with a candle, and Wise Owl flew down to inspect them.

"Very good work," said he. "You are artists now. I will hang these over my bookcase. I shall look at the little house and know you are safe inside because the candle is burning. I shall look at the plate of cakes and I need not go a-hunting. There's plenty to eat."

He flew back to his tree and hung the pictures on the wall, but he had to go hunting after all as Squirrel's cakes were not good to eat. However, it made him happy to look at them.

Hare stepped softly through the garden gate and he stuck his picture to a tree so that the Fox would find it. He heard a rustle, and he scampered back as fast as he could go. When he was safe in the garden he turned round. There was the Fox staring at his picture in the moonlight, turning it upside down and every way.

"Thank you, Hare, artist," cried the Fox. "A good likeness in every direction. I am glad to see you are so anxious to have supper with me that you are riding on my back. Let it be soon! Roast hare and redcurrant jelly!"

Hare didn't wait to explain. He dashed indoors and drew the bolts.

"The Fox didn't understand my picture after all," he told Grey Rabbit.

"Never mind, Hare. We are all artists now, and sometimes real artists aren't understood," said Grey Rabbit, soothing him. "You are a clever Hare and you painted the Fox."

They ate their supper and then they looked out of the window to say "Goodnight" to the moon.

"Goodnight, Moon," they called, bowing their little heads, and a silvery music answered from the heavens,

"Goodnight, small animals. Goodnight."

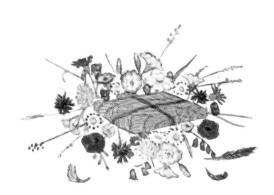